U0005430

THE
VELVETEEN
RABBIT

OR HOW TOYS
BECOME REAL

by **Margery Williams**

with illustrations by **William Nicholson**

CONTENT

1

Christmas
Morning

THERE was once a velveteen rabbit, and in the beginning he was really splendid. He was fat and bunchy, as a rabbit should be; his coat was spotted brown and white, he had real thread whiskers, and his ears were lined with pink sateen. On Christmas morning, when he sat wedged in the top of the Boy's stocking, with a sprig of holly between his paws, the effect was charming.

There were other things in the stocking, nuts and oranges and a toy engine, and chocolate almonds and a clockwork mouse, but the Rabbit was quite the best of all. For at least two hours the Boy loved him, and then Aunts and Uncles came to dinner, and there was a great rustling of tissue paper and unwrapping of parcels, and in the excitement of looking at all the new presents the Velveteen Rabbit was forgotten.

For a long time he lived in the toy cupboard or on the nursery floor, and no one thought very much about him. He was naturally shy, and being only made of velveteen, some of the more expensive toys quite snubbed him. The mechanical toys were very superior, and looked down upon everyone else; they were full of modern ideas, and pretended they were real. The model boat, who had lived through two seasons and lost most of his paint, caught the tone from them and never missed an opportunity of referring to his rigging in technical terms. The Rabbit could not claim to be a model of anything, for he didn't know that real rabbits existed; he thought they were all stuffed with sawdust like himself, and he understood that sawdust was quite out-of-date and should never be mentioned in modern circles. Even Timothy, the jointed wooden lion, who was made by the disabled soldiers, and should have had broader views, put on airs and pretended he was connected with Government. Between them all the poor little Rabbit was made to feel himself very insignificant and commonplace, and the only person who was kind to him at all was the Skin Horse.

The Skin Horse had lived longer in the nursery than any of the others. He was so old that his brown coat was bald in patches and showed the seams underneath, and most of the hairs in his tail had been pulled out to string bead necklaces. He was wise, for he had seen a long succession of mechanical toys arrive to boast and swagger, and by-and-by break their mainsprings and pass away, and he knew that they were only toys, and would never turn into anything else. For nursery magic is very strange and wonderful, and only those playthings that are old and wise and experienced like the Skin Horse understand all about it.

"What is **REAL**?" asked the Rabbit one day, when they were lying side by side near the nursery fender, before Nana came to tidy the room. "Does it mean having things that buzz inside you and a stick-out handle?"

"Real isn't how you are made," said the Skin Horse. "It's a thing that happens to you. When a child loves you for a long, long time, not just to play with, but **REALLY** loves you, then you become Real."

"Does it hurt?" asked the Rabbit.

"Sometimes," said the Skin Horse, for he was always truthful. "When you are Real you don't mind being hurt."

"Does it happen all at once, like being wound up," he asked, "or bit by bit?"

"It doesn't happen all at once," said the Skin Horse. "You become. It takes a long time. That's why it doesn't happen often to people who break easily, or have sharp edges, or who have to be carefully kept. Generally, by the time you are Real, most of your hair has been loved off, and your eyes drop out and you get loose in the joints and very shabby. But these things don't matter at all, because once you are Real you can't be ugly, except to people who don't understand."

"I suppose *you* are real?" said the Rabbit. And then he wished he had not said it, for he thought the Skin Horse might be sensitive. But the Skin Horse only smiled.

"The Boy's Uncle made me Real," he said. "That was a great many years ago; but once you are Real you can't become unreal again. It lasts for always."

The Rabbit sighed. He thought it would be a long time before this magic called Real happened to him. He longed to become Real, to know what it felt like; and yet the idea of growing shabby and losing his eyes and whiskers was rather sad. He wished that he could become it without these uncomfortable things happening to him.

2

Spring
Time

There was a person called Nana who ruled the nursery. Sometimes she took no notice of the playthings lying about, and sometimes, for no reason whatever, she went swooping about like a great wind and hustled them away in cupboards. She called this "tidying up," and the playthings all hated it, especially the tin ones. The Rabbit didn't mind it so much, for wherever he was thrown he came down soft.

One evening, when the Boy was going to bed, he couldn't find the china dog that always slept with him. Nana was in a hurry, and it was too much trouble to hunt for china dogs at bedtime, so she simply looked about her, and seeing that the toy cupboard door stood open, she made a swoop.

"Here," she said, "take your old Bunny! He'll do to sleep with you!" And she dragged the Rabbit out by one ear, and put him into the Boy's arms.

That night, and for many nights after, the Velveteen Rabbit slept in the Boy's bed. At first he found it rather uncomfortable, for the Boy hugged him very tight, and sometimes he rolled over on him, and sometimes he pushed him so far under the pillow that the Rabbit could scarcely breathe. And he missed, too, those long moonlight hours in the nursery, when all the house was silent, and his talks with the Skin Horse. But very soon he grew to like it, for the Boy used to talk to him, and made nice tunnels for him under the bedclothes that he said were like the burrows the real rabbits lived in. And they had splendid games together, in whispers, when Nana had gone away to her supper and left the night-light burning on the mantelpiece. And when the Boy dropped off to sleep, the Rabbit would snuggle down close under his little warm chin and dream, with the Boy's hands clasped close round him all night long.

And so time went on, and the little Rabbit was very happy–so happy that he never noticed how his beautiful velveteen fur was getting shabbier and shabbier, and his tail becoming unsewn, and all the pink rubbed off his nose where the Boy had kissed him.

Spring came, and they had long days in the garden, for wherever the Boy went the Rabbit went too. He had rides in the wheelbarrow, and picnics on the grass, and lovely fairy huts built for him under the raspberry canes behind the flower border. And once, when the Boy was called away suddenly to go out to tea, the Rabbit was left out on the lawn until long after dusk, and Nana had to come and look for him with the candle because the Boy couldn't go to sleep unless he was there. He was wet through with the dew and quite earthy from diving into the burrows the Boy had made for him in the flower bed, and Nana grumbled as she rubbed him off with a corner of her apron.

"You must have your old Bunny!" she said. "Fancy all that fuss for a toy!"

The Boy sat up in bed and stretched out his hands.

"Give me my Bunny!" he said. "You mustn't say that. He isn't a toy. He's **REAL!**"

When the little Rabbit heard that he was happy, for he knew that what the Skin Horse had said was true at last. The nursery magic had happened to him, and he was a toy no longer. He was Real. The Boy himself had said it.

That night he was almost too happy to sleep, and so much love stirred in his little sawdust heart that it almost burst. And into his boot-button eyes, that had long ago lost their polish, there came a look of wisdom and beauty, so that even Nana noticed it next morning when she picked him up, and said, "I declare if that old Bunny hasn't got quite a knowing expression!"

3

Summer

That was a wonderful Summer!

Near the house where they lived there was a wood, and in the long June evenings the Boy liked to go there after tea to play. He took the Velveteen Rabbit with him, and before he wandered off to pick flowers, or play at brigands among the trees, he always made the Rabbit a little nest somewhere among the bracken, where he would be quite cosy, for he was a kind-hearted little boy and he liked Bunny to be comfortable. One evening, while the Rabbit was lying there alone, watching the ants that ran to and fro between his velvet paws in the grass, he saw two strange beings creep out of the tall bracken near him.

They were rabbits like himself, but quite furry and brand-new. They must have been very well made, for their seams didn't show at all, and they changed shape in a queer way when they moved; one minute they were long and thin and the next minute fat and bunchy, instead of always staying the same like he did. Their feet padded softly on the ground, and they crept quite close to him, twitching their noses, while the Rabbit stared hard to see which side the clockwork stuck out, for he knew that people who jump generally have something to wind them up. But he couldn't see it. They were evidently a new kind of rabbit altogether.

They stared at him, and the little Rabbit stared back. And all the time their noses twitched.

"Why don't you get up and play with us?" one of them asked.

"I don't feel like it," said the Rabbit, for he didn't want to explain that he had no clockwork.

"Ho!" said the furry rabbit. "It's as easy as anything," And he gave a big hop sideways and stood on his hind legs.

"I don't believe you can!" he said.

"I can!" said the little Rabbit. "I can jump higher than anything!" He meant when the Boy threw him, but of course he didn't want to say so.

"Can you hop on your hind legs?" asked the furry rabbit.

That was a dreadful question, for the Velveteen Rabbit had no hind legs at all! The back of him was made all in one piece, like a pincushion. He sat still in the bracken, and hoped that the other rabbits wouldn't notice.

"I don't want to!" he said again.

But the wild rabbits have very sharp eyes. And this one stretched out his neck and looked.

"He hasn't got any hind legs!" he called out. "Fancy a rabbit without any hind legs!" And he began to laugh.

"I have!" cried the little Rabbit. "I have got hind legs! I am sitting on them!"

"Then stretch them out and show me, like this!" said the wild rabbit. And he began to whirl round and dance, till the little Rabbit got quite dizzy.

"I don't like dancing," he said. "I'd rather sit still!"

But all the while he was longing to dance, for a funny new tickly feeling ran through him, and he felt he would give anything in the world to be able to jump about like these rabbits did.

The strange rabbit stopped dancing, and came quite close. He came so close this time that his long whiskers brushed the Velveteen Rabbit's ear, and then he wrinkled his nose suddenly and flattened his ears and jumped backwards.

"He doesn't smell right!" he exclaimed. "He isn't a rabbit at all! He isn't real!"

"I *am* Real!" said the little Rabbit. "I am Real! The Boy said so!" And he nearly began to cry.

Just then there was a sound of footsteps, and the Boy ran past near them, and with a stamp of feet and a flash of white tails the two strange rabbits disappeared.

"Come back and play with me!" called the little Rabbit. "Oh, do come back! I *know* I am Real!"

But there was no answer, only the little ants ran to and fro, and the bracken swayed gently where the two strangers had passed. The Velveteen Rabbit was all alone.

"Oh, dear!" he thought. "Why did they run away like that? Why couldn't they stop and talk to me?"

For a long time he lay very still, watching the bracken, and hoping that they would come back. But they never returned, and presently the sun sank lower and the little white moths fluttered out, and the Boy came and carried him home.

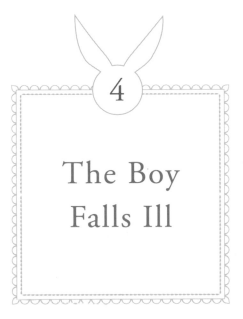

4

The Boy
Falls Ill

Weeks passed, and the little Rabbit grew very old and shabby, but the Boy loved him just as much. He loved him so hard that he loved all his whiskers off, and the pink lining to his ears turned grey, and his brown spots faded. He even began to lose his shape, and he scarcely looked like a rabbit anymore, except to the Boy. To him he was always beautiful, and that was all that the little Rabbit cared about. He didn't mind how he looked to other people, because the nursery magic had made him Real, and when you are Real shabbiness doesn't matter.

And then, one day, the Boy was ill.

His face grew very flushed, and he talked in his sleep, and his little body was so hot that it burned the Rabbit when he held him close. Strange people came and went in the nursery, and a light burned all night and through it all the little Velveteen Rabbit lay there, hidden from sight under the bedclothes, and he never stirred, for he was afraid that if they found him someone might take him away, and he knew that the Boy needed him.

It was a long weary time, for the Boy was too ill to play, and the little Rabbit found it rather dull with nothing to do all day long. But he snuggled down patiently, and looked forward to the time when the Boy should be well again, and they would go out in the garden amongst the flowers and the butterflies and play splendid games in the raspberry thicket like they used to. All sorts of delightful things he planned, and while the Boy lay half asleep he crept up close to the pillow and whispered them in his ear. And presently the fever turned, and the Boy got better. He was able to sit up in bed and look at picture-books, while the little Rabbit cuddled close at his side. And one day, they let him get up and dress.

It was a bright, sunny morning, and the windows stood wide

open. They had carried the Boy out on to the balcony, wrapped in a shawl, and the little Rabbit lay tangled up among the bedclothes, thinking.

The Boy was going to the seaside tomorrow. Everything was arranged, and now it only remained to carry out the doctor's orders. They talked about it all, while the little Rabbit lay under the bedclothes, with just his head peeping out, and listened. The room was to be disinfected, and all the books and toys that the Boy had played with in bed must be burnt.

"Hurrah!" thought the little Rabbit. "Tomorrow we shall go to the seaside!" For the boy had often talked of the seaside, and he wanted very much to see the big waves coming in, and the tiny crabs, and the sand castles.

Just then Nana caught sight of him.

"How about his old Bunny?" she asked.

"*That* ?" said the doctor. "Why, it's a mass of scarlet fever germs!–Burn it at once. What? Nonsense! Get him a new one. He mustn't have that anymore!"

5

Anxious
Times

And so the little Rabbit was put into a sack with the old picture-books and a lot of rubbish, and carried out to the end of the garden behind the fowl-house. That was a fine place to make a bonfire, only the gardener was too busy just then to attend to it. He had the potatoes to dig and the green peas to gather, but next morning he promised to come quite early and burn the whole lot.

That night the Boy slept in a different bedroom, and he had a new bunny to sleep with him. It was a splendid bunny, all white plush with real glass eyes, but the Boy was too excited to care very much about it. For tomorrow he was going to the seaside, and that in itself was such a wonderful thing that he could think of nothing else.

And while the Boy was asleep, dreaming of the seaside, the little Rabbit lay among the old picture-books in the corner behind the fowl-house, and he felt very lonely. The sack had been left untied, and so by wriggling a bit he was able to get his head through the opening and look out. He was shivering a little, for he had always been used to sleeping in a proper bed, and by this time his coat had worn so thin and threadbare from hugging that it was no longer any protection to him. Nearby he could see the thicket of raspberry canes, growing tall and close like a tropical jungle, in whose shadow he had played with the Boy on bygone mornings. He thought of those long sunlit hours in the garden–how happy thcy wcrc–and a great sadness came over him. He seemed to see them all pass before him, each more beautiful than the other, the fairy huts in the flower-bed, the quiet evenings in the wood when he lay in the bracken and the little ants ran over his paws; the wonderful day when he first knew that he was Real. He thought of the Skin Horse, so wise and gentle, and all that he had told him. Of what use was it to be loved and lose one's beauty and become Real if it all ended like this? And a tear, a real tear, trickled down his little shabby velvet nose and fell to the ground.

And then a strange thing happened. For where the tear had fallen a flower grew out of the ground, a mysterious flower, not at all like any that grew in the garden. It had slender green leaves the colour of emeralds, and in the centre of the leaves a blossom like a golden cup. It was so beautiful that the little Rabbit forgot to cry, and just lay there watching it. And presently the blossom opened, and out of it there stepped a fairy.

6

The
Fairy

She was quite the loveliest fairy in the whole world. Her dress was of pearl and dew-drops, and there were flowers round her neck and in her hair, and her face was like the most perfect flower of all. And she came close to the little Rabbit and gathered him up in her arms and kissed him on his velveteen nose that was all damp from crying.

"Little Rabbit," she said, "don't you know who I am?"

The Rabbit looked up at her, and it seemed to him that he had seen her face before, but he couldn't think where.

"I am the nursery magic Fairy," she said. "I take care of all the playthings that the children have loved. When they are old and worn out and the children don't need them anymore, then I come and take them away with me and turn them into Real."

"Wasn't I Real before?" asked the little Rabbit.

"You were Real to the Boy," the Fairy said, "because he loved you. Now you shall be Real to everyone."

And she held the little Rabbit close in her arms and flew with him into the wood.

It was light now, for the moon had risen. All the forest was beautiful, and the fronds of the bracken shone like frosted silver. In the open glade between the tree-trunks the wild rabbits danced with their shadows on the velvet grass, but when they saw the Fairy they all stopped dancing and stood round in a ring to stare at her.

"I've brought you a new playfellow," the Fairy said. "You must be very kind to him and teach him all he needs to know in

Rabbit-land, for he is going to live with you for ever and ever!"

And she kissed the little Rabbit again and put him down on the grass.

"Run and play, little Rabbit!" she said.

But the little Rabbit sat quite still for a moment and never moved. For when he saw all the wild rabbits dancing around him he suddenly remembered about his hind legs, and he didn't want them to see that he was made all in one piece. He did not know that when the Fairy kissed him that last time she had changed him altogether. And he might have sat there a long time, too shy to move, if just then something hadn't tickled his nose, and before he thought what he was doing he lifted his hind toe to scratch it.

And he found that he actually had hind legs! Instead of dingy velveteen he had brown fur, soft and shiny, his ears twitched by themselves, and his whiskers were so long that they brushed the grass. He gave one leap and the joy of using those hind legs was so great that he went springing about the turf on them, jumping sideways and whirling round as the others did, and he grew so excited that when at last he did stop to look for the Fairy she had gone.

He was a Real Rabbit at last, at home with the other rabbits.

Autumn passed and Winter, and in the Spring, when the days grew warm and sunny, the Boy went out to play in the wood behind the house. And while he was playing, two rabbits crept out from the bracken and peeped at him. One of them was brown all over, but the other had strange markings under his fur, as though long ago he had been spotted, and the spots still showed through. And about his little soft nose and his round black eyes there was something familiar, so that the Boy thought to himself:

"Why, he looks just like my old Bunny that was lost when I had scarlet fever!"

But he never knew that it really was his own Bunny, come back to look at the child who had first helped him to be Real.

天鵝絨毛兔

瑪格利・威廉斯————著

劉清彥——譯　恩佐——繪

愛經典 018

天鵝絨毛兔
【珍藏獨家夜光版】（中英雙語）
THE VELVETEEN RABBIT

作者 瑪格利．威廉斯 Margery Williams ｜**繪者** 恩佐｜**譯者** 劉清彥
出版者 愛米粒出版有限公司｜**地址** 台北市 10445 中山北路二段 26 巷 2 號
2 樓｜**編輯部專線**（02）2562-2159｜**傳真**（02）2581-8761
如果您對本書或本出版公司有任何意見，歡迎來電

總編輯 莊靜君｜**美術設計** 王瓊瑤｜**行銷企劃** 李嘉琪｜**中文校對** 金文蕙、徐
惠蓉｜**英文校對** 翁家怡｜**行政編輯** 曾于珊｜**印刷** 上好印刷股份有限公司｜
電話（04）23150280｜**初版** 二〇二一年（民 110）二月十日｜**定價** 250 元｜
總經銷 知己圖書股份有限公司｜**郵政劃撥** 15060393｜（台北公司）台北
市 106 辛亥路一段 30 號 9 樓　**電話：**（02）2367-2044／2367-2047　**傳真：**
（02）2363-5741｜（台中公司）台中市 407 工業 30 路 1 號　**電話：**
（04）2359-5819　**傳真：**（04）2359-5493｜**法律顧問** 陳思成
國際書碼 978-986 99917-1-1　**CIP** 874.596/109021013

愛米粒出版

因為閱讀，我們放膽作夢，恣意飛翔。
在看書成了非必要奢侈品，文學小說式微的年代，
愛米粒堅持出版好看的故事，讓世界多一點想像力，多一點希望。

愛米粒FB

填寫線上回函卡
送購書優惠券

目錄

真正的兔子，真正的人

◎劉清彥

一九○二年深秋，英國著名的兒童文學作家和插畫家碧雅翠絲・波特女士筆下那隻調皮搗蛋的「小兔彼得」，蹦蹦跳跳躍進倫敦書店，也從此躍上兒童文學的經典地位。二十年後，隔洋對岸的美國也出現了兒童文學史上的另一隻經典兔子，這隻由美國作家瑪格利・威廉斯女士一手打造的「天鵝絨毛兔」，出場雖不及小兔

彼得亮眼討喜（一如他在故事中毫不起眼的模樣和處境），卻以他

真實深刻的動人情感，和極具廣度與深度的思維啟發，觸動並震撼

許多人的心，這股強烈的衝擊力道近一百年來歷久不減。

這隻絨毛兔為什麼有如此大的威力呢？表面看來，這個故事揉

合了安徒生《人魚公主》為愛犧牲和柯洛迪《木偶奇遇記》由假成

真的童話元素，似乎不見新意，然而，威廉斯女士擺脫了悲劇浪

漫和教條傳統，將故事的光圈焦點投射在關涉生命意義、價值和成

長等與每個人切身相關的心理舞台，藉由這隻渴望愛與成真的絨毛

兔，把人（不管是大人或小孩）最內在的情感和需求掏出來，使這

隻絨毛兔在讀者翻閱書頁的剎那，就輕巧地跳進他們心房，激盪心思和情感。

其實許多人心裡都藏著這麼一隻絨毛兔：不敢面對自己的軟弱或缺陷，又容易在膚淺的世俗較量中敗陣，因而自我形象日益偏差薄弱，甚至懷疑自己存在的價值。他們希望被愛，也期許自己有愛人的能力，卻因為裹足不前或過度自我保護，和真愛失之交臂，無法體驗真正的幸福。所以，威廉斯女士便藉由這隻絨毛兔，呈現人的成長困境和疑慮，也透過充滿想像、信心、希望、平和又美好的故事結局，為身處困局的人指引出路。

作者在書中以「真假」的辯證，提醒讀者思考生命中最重要的是什麼。天鵝絨毛兔遇見仙子前，雖然在客觀真實的認定中仍是隻假兔子，卻因為男孩的愛使他重拾自信和自尊，並且相信自己是真的，有了這樣真實的愛和關懷，就算外貌漸殘也不以為意。作者著眼的不是絨毛兔因為乖巧美麗或表現良好才變成真的，而是因為愛與被愛使自己踏上自我重塑的過程，最後終於美夢成真。表相的虛假對應內在情感的真實，支持生命最重要的元素也不言自喻。

正因為這個故事有多層次的心理意涵，便有心理學家由此發展出「絨毛兔的心理治療處方」。他們從故事中提煉「成真要

008

素」（例如：愛、同情、勇氣、誠實、慷慨、感恩、挫折容忍和同理心……等），透過故事幫助許多大人小孩發展「自我同情」

（self-empathy）的能力，以寬容的態度接受自己的侷限和缺陷，用新的眼光看待自己，活出真正的自己。就像美國一位心理醫師Toni Raiten-D'antonio 所言：「『成真』是許多心理治療所要達成的目的，這表示人能夠自我尊重與尊重他人，並且真實地表現自我，勇於面對生活中的壓力、衝突、悲傷和失落，使我們成為仁慈、善良又正直的人。」

「絨毛兔」的故事脫胎自威廉斯女士的幼年成長經驗，書中

的主角正是她的第一個玩具，一隻名叫托比（Tubby）的天鵝絨毛兔，而那隻滿有智慧和閱歷豐富的「真皮馬」則是她幼年最喜愛的玩具。威廉斯女士坦言，這些玩具在她眼中都是有生命的真實個體，因為她愛他們，他們也是陪伴她成長的重要夥伴。

威廉斯女士從小生長在充滿愛與關懷、自由又開放的家庭，她擔任律師的父親相信，學校的正規教育會框限小孩的思想和心靈，使小孩失去該有的天真、想像與創造力，因此威廉斯女士從小接受在家教育。或許正因為有家人堅實穩固的關愛基礎，和未曾受約制的自由心靈，使她能創作出這樣動人深沉的經典故事。這個

010

故事雖為小孩而寫，但是她希望閱讀故事的大人和小孩不僅能被愛，並且透過充滿愛的關係成為「真正的人」。

絨毛兔與男孩的情誼感動，也能從中學習接納自己，相信自己值得被愛，並且透過充滿愛的關係成為「真正的人」。

1

玩ㄨㄢˊ具ㄐㄩˋ要ㄧㄠˋ如ㄖㄨˊ何ㄏㄜˊ
才ㄘㄞˊ會ㄏㄨㄟˋ變ㄅㄧㄢˋ成ㄔㄥˊ真ㄓㄣ的˙ㄉㄜ？

從前有隻天鵝絨毛兔，他原本漂亮極了，圓圓胖胖、蓬鬆柔軟，就像隻兔子該有的模樣；他的絨毛上有棕色和白色斑點，鬍鬚用細線做成，耳朵還有緞帶襯裡。聖誕節早晨，他被塞在男孩襪子的最上面，冬青枝子正好繞過他的腳掌間，使他看起來非常迷人。

襪子裡還有別的東西，胡桃、橘子、玩具火車、杏仁巧克力和發條老鼠，但絨毛兔是其中最棒的，因為男孩至少有兩小時對他愛不釋手。然後，叔叔阿姨們紛紛來吃晚餐，一時間，屋裡充滿撕包裝紙和拆包裹的沙沙聲響，男孩興奮地看著每樣新禮物，遺忘了絨毛兔。

絨毛兔在玩具櫃和育兒室的地板上待了很長一段時間，沒有人注意他。他生性害羞，又只是用天鵝絨布做成的玩偶，有些昂貴的玩具就瞧不起他。那些精美的機械玩具常常輕視其他玩具；他們身上充滿新奇的設計，而且自以為就是真的。像那艘模型船雖然已經兩年，身上的漆也快掉光了，卻還是洋洋得意，絕不會錯失用專業術語展現自己精良裝備的機會。絨毛兔稱不上是模型，因為他不知道真的兔子長什麼樣子；他以為所有的兔子都像他，體內塞滿木屑，他也知道木屑早就過時了，在這些時髦玩具面前千萬不能提。即使是那隻用壞掉的士兵玩偶做成、名叫提摩太的木頭組合獅

016

子，也跟著裝腔作勢，假裝自己就是高高在上的統治者（他的眼光

應該比較開闊才對）。夾在他們中間，可憐的小絨毛兔覺得自己

平凡無奇，一點都不起眼，唯一對他仁慈和善的只有那隻真皮馬。

真皮馬是育兒室裡最長壽的玩具，他實在太老了，身上的棕

色皮面有些地方已經被磨光，連接縫線都露出來，尾巴上大多數的

毛也被拔去串項鍊。不過，他很有智慧，他看多了這些機械玩具誇

耀吹噓、大搖大擺地來，又一個個被拆毀發條，然後丟棄，他知道

他們只是玩具，絕對不可能變成真的東西。因為育兒室魔法神奇又

美妙，只有像真皮馬這樣年老、經驗豐富又充滿智慧的玩具才能

通曉一切。「什麼是『真的』？」有一天，在娜娜進來整理房間前，他們肩並肩躺在育兒室的防護板附近，絨毛兔開口問。「是不是變成真的以後，你就會有一根凸出來的旋鈕，身體裡面還會有東西發出嗡嗡嗡的聲音？」

「才不是你想的那樣，」真皮馬說。「變成真的表示有件事會發生在你身上。如果有個小孩愛你很久很久，不只是跟你玩，而是

『真的』很愛你，你就會變成真的了。」

「會痛嗎？」絨毛兔問。

「有時候會，」真皮馬誠實地回答。「但是你變成真的以後，

天鵝絨毛兔

就不會在意那種痛了。」

「它會突然發生，像上緊發條那樣，」他又問，「還是一點一點出現？」

「不會突然發生，」真皮馬說。「你會漸漸改變，那需要很長的時間。所以這件事不常發生在那些容易損壞、有尖銳稜角、或是必須好好保存的玩具身上。一般來說，在你變成真的以後，身上大多數的毛會因為一直被擁抱而脫落，你的眼睛會掉下來，身上的縫合處會鬆開，變得又髒又破。可是那完全不重要，因為一旦你變成真的，除了那些不了解你的人以外，不會有人嫌你醜。」

　天鵝絨毛兔

「我想，你應該已經變成真的了，對不對？」絨毛兔才說出

口就後悔了，他真希望自己沒有說這句話，因為真皮馬可能很敏

感。但真皮馬只是笑一笑。

「是男孩的叔叔讓我變成真的，」他說。「那是好幾年前的

事了；而且你變成真的以後，就不會再變回假的了。永遠都是真

的。」

絨毛兔嘆了口氣，他心裡想，大概得經過很長的時間，這個

「成真」的魔法才會發生在自己身上。他渴望變成真的，很想知道

那是種什麼樣的感覺；雖然一想到自己會變得又髒又破，也會失去

022

眼睛和鬍鬚，還是很難過。他希望自己變成真的，又不希望發生那些不幸的事。

天鵝絨毛兔

2

絨ㄖㄨㄥˊ毛ㄇㄠˊ兔ㄊㄨˋ
遇ㄩˋ見ㄐㄧㄢˋ小ㄒㄧㄠˇ男ㄋㄢˊ孩ㄏㄞˊ

負責打掃育兒室的人名叫娜娜，有時候她根本不會留意玩具們躺在哪裡，但有時候，也不曉得為什麼，她會像狂風似的撲向那些玩具，把他們撿起來塞進櫃子。她說自己是在「整理」，玩具們卻很討厭她這麼做，尤其是那些小錫兵。絨毛兔倒不太在意，因為不管他被扔在哪裡，掉下來時都不會痛。

有天晚上，男孩上床前怎麼也找不到平常陪他睡覺的小瓷狗。娜娜很不耐煩，就要睡覺了，還得去找小瓷狗，實在太麻煩了。於是，她只是四處瞧瞧，發現玩具櫃的門還開著，就急忙衝過去。

「拿去，」她說，「抱著你這隻舊兔子吧！他會陪你睡覺！」娜娜揪著絨毛兔的一隻耳朵，把他塞進男孩懷裡。

那天晚上和接下來的許多天晚上，絨毛兔就一直睡在男孩的床上。

剛開始他覺得很不舒服，因為男孩把他抱得好緊好緊，有時翻過身子壓著他，有時把他推到枕頭下面，害他差點喘不過氣來。

他也懷念育兒室裡充滿月光的漫長夜晚，他和真皮馬在一片寂靜中愉快聊天的時光。可是沒多久，他就開始喜歡陪男孩睡覺了，因為男孩常常跟他說話，還在棉被下面為他做了很棒的坑道，男孩說，這樣他就有個真正的兔子洞穴了。在娜娜留下壁爐台上的小夜

028

燈、離開房間去吃晚餐後，他們就會一起玩有趣的遊戲，輕聲細語交談。男孩睡著了，絨毛兔就靠在他溫暖的小下巴，讓男孩的手整夜緊緊抱著他，進入夢鄉。

日子一天天過去，小絨毛兔真的很快樂，他完全沒有發現自己漂亮的絨毛變得越來越骯髒，越來越破舊，尾巴開始脫線，就連原本粉紅色的鼻子也因為被男孩不斷親吻而掉色了。

春天到了，他們整天在花園玩耍，不管男孩去哪裡都帶著絨毛兔。他坐著獨輪手推車兜風，在草地上野餐，男孩甚至還在花圃後方的覆盆子叢下面，為他蓋了間可愛的小茅屋。有一次，男孩

　天鵝絨毛兔

突然被叫去喝茶，把絨毛兔遺忘在草地上，直到天色變暗，娜娜才點著蠟燭來找他，因為沒有他，男孩就不肯睡覺。他的身體被露水浸濕了，還因為在男孩挖的洞穴裡待了太久，全身充滿濃濃的泥土味，娜娜一邊抱怨，一邊拎起圍裙的一角，把他擦乾淨。

「你非要這隻又老又舊的兔子不可嗎？」她說。「為了個玩具大驚小怪，實在太離譜了！」

男孩從床上坐起來，伸出手。

「把兔兔給我！」他說，「妳不能這樣說他，他才不是玩具呢，他是『真』的！」

小兔子聽見這句話，心裡高興極了，他知道真皮馬說的事終於發生了。育兒室魔法靈驗了，他已經不再是玩具，他是真的了，男孩親口說的。

那天晚上，他高興得睡不著，那顆小小的木屑心中充滿了愛，幾乎就要脹破，而且在他那雙早已變得灰暗的黑眼睛裡，彷彿還閃爍一點點美與智慧的光彩，就連娜娜在第二天早晨撿起他時也察覺到了，她說：「這隻老兔子看起來還真有點聰明呢！」

034

3

我是真的嗎？

多美好的夏天啊！

在他們住的房子附近有座森林，整個冗長的六月傍晚，男孩總是喜歡在喝過午茶後去那裡玩。他帶著絨毛兔一起去，在他開始到處摘花或穿梭林間玩官兵捉強盜的遊戲前，都會在蕨類叢生的地方為絨毛兔做個小窩，讓他舒服地休息，因為他是個心地善良的小男孩，希望他的兔兔覺得很舒服。有天傍晚，絨毛兔獨自躺著休息，看著成群螞蟻在他絨毛腳掌間的青草上跑來跑去時，發現兩隻奇怪的生物爬出高大的蕨類，漸漸靠近他。

他們看起來和他很像，只是毛比較蓬鬆，也比較新。他們一定

被做得很精美，因為他們的縫線完全沒有露出來，而且活動時，身體的形狀也會出現奇怪的變化；一會兒又細又長，一會兒又蓬又胖，不像他永遠保持不變。他們的腳輕輕在地上蹬蹬跳跳，靠近他身邊，抽動鼻子嗅聞著。絨毛兔仔細在他們身上尋找凸出來的發條旋鈕，他知道那些會跳動的玩具身上都有這種裝置。但是他怎麼也找不到，顯然他們是一種新的兔子。

他們盯著絨毛兔，絨毛兔也盯著他們，大家都抽動鼻子聞來聞去。

「你為什麼不起來和我們玩？」其中一隻兔子問。

「我不喜歡玩，」絨毛兔說，因為他不想讓他們知道自己沒有發條。

「哦！」毛茸茸的兔子說。「很好玩啊。」說完，他就高高跳向一旁，用後腿站著。

「你一定辦不到！」他說。

「我可以！」絨毛兔說。「我能跳得比任何東西還要高！」

他是指男孩把他高高拋起來的時候，可是他當然不想這麼說。

「你能用後腿跳躍嗎？」毛茸茸的兔子問。

那真是個要命的問題，因為絨毛兔根本沒有後腿！他的底部被

039　　天鵝絨毛兔

縫成一整塊，像個針插。他靜靜坐在蕨類上，希望那兩隻兔子不會發現這件事。

「我不想這麼做！」他又說。

不過，野兔的眼睛非常銳利，其中一隻伸長脖子仔細看著他。

「他沒有後腿！」他大聲說。「沒有後腿的兔子，多奇怪啊！」他哈哈大笑起來。「我有！」小絨毛兔大叫。「我有後腿！我正坐在它們上面！」

「伸出來給我看看哪，像這樣！」野兔說，他開始不停地旋轉

和跳舞，直到小絨毛兔看得頭都暈了。

「我不喜歡跳舞，」他說。「我寧可靜靜地坐著。」

其實，他一直很想跳舞。絨毛兔心中充滿了一種新鮮有趣的感覺，他願意付出一切代價，只要能像這兩隻兔子一樣跳躍就好了。

陌生的兔子不再跳舞了，他靠近絨毛兔身邊，靠得很近很近，長長的鬍鬚碰觸到絨毛兔的耳朵，然後他突然皺起鼻子，壓低耳朵，往後一跳。

「他的味道不對！」他驚叫。「他根本不是兔子！他不是真

的！」

「我是真的！」小絨毛兔說。「我是真的！是男孩說的！」

他差點哭出來。

就在那時候，出現了腳步聲，男孩從他們旁邊跑過去，一蹬腳，兩團白尾巴一閃而過，陌生的兔子消失得無影無蹤。

「回來呀，跟我一起玩嘛！」絨毛兔大喊。「快回來啊！我知道我是真的！」

可是沒有回應，只看見小螞蟻來回穿梭，還有陌生兔子剛剛跳過的地方、蕨類輕輕搖擺晃動。絨毛兔又落單了。

「哎呀！」他心裡想。「他們為什麼能像那樣跑開？為什麼不肯停下來和我聊天呢？」

他靜靜地坐了很久，看著身旁的蕨類，希望他們會回來，但是他們沒有回來。太陽漸漸西沉，小白蛾拍打翅膀，飛來飛去。男孩來了，帶他一起回家。

044

4

小男孩生病了

幾星期過去了，小絨毛兔雖然變得又髒又舊，男孩卻更愛他。

男孩好愛好愛絨毛兔，因為太用力抱他，使他的鬍鬚脫落了，耳朵的粉紅色襯裡變成灰灰的，身上的棕色斑點也漸漸褪色。他的模樣和形狀甚至和從前不同，看起來再也不像隻兔子。只有男孩對他的感覺沒變，在男孩眼中，他一直很美麗，那也是小絨毛兔最在意的事。他不在乎別人的看法，因為育兒室魔法已經讓他變成真的了，而且只要你是真的，就算變得又髒又舊也沒有關係。

直到有一天，男孩生病了。

他的臉紅通通的，昏睡時喃喃自語，小小的身體熱得發燙，

他緊緊抱著絨毛兔時，連絨毛兔也熱得受不了。陌生人在育兒室來來去去，夜晚的房間裡總是點著一盞小燈，只有小絨毛兔躺在床上陪伴男孩，他躲在棉被下面，不敢亂動，因為他害怕被人發現，然後把他帶走，他知道男孩現在很需要他。

那是一段又長又悶的時間，因為男孩病得太嚴重，沒辦法和他一起玩，小絨毛兔發現，一整天沒事可做，實在太無聊了。不過，他還是很有耐心地靠在男孩身邊，希望男孩早日康復，再和他一起到花園，像從前一樣，在花叢中追蝴蝶，在覆盆子叢裡玩有趣的遊戲。他計畫了各種好玩的事，趁男孩半睡半醒時，偷偷爬上枕頭，

在他耳邊輕聲告訴他。

男孩的病情漸漸好轉，高燒慢慢退了，他已經可以坐在床上，一邊抱著絨毛兔，一邊看圖畫書。有一天，大人們終於讓他下床，為他換衣服。

那是個陽光燦爛的早晨，窗戶大大敞開，他們為男孩披上披肩，帶他去陽台，小絨毛兔躺在棉被堆裡想事情。

男孩明天要去海邊呢！一切都安排妥當，只要得到醫生的許可就行了。他們一直在談論這件事，小絨毛兔靜靜躺在棉被下面，探出頭偷看、偷聽。這個房間必須好好消毒，所有的書和男孩在床上玩過的玩具都得燒掉。

「太棒了！」小絨毛兔心裡想。「明天我們就能一起去海邊！」

男孩常常提到海邊，他很想去看看大浪拍打岸邊的情景，也想看看小螃蟹，在沙灘堆城堡。

就在那時候，娜娜瞥見絨毛兔。

「這隻又破又舊的兔子該怎麼辦？」她問。

「哪隻？」醫生說。「呃，上面一定有很多猩紅熱的病菌！馬上燒掉。什麼，別開玩笑了！買隻新的給他，他不許再碰那隻兔子了！」

　天鵝絨毛兔

5

小兔子的眼淚

於是，小絨毛兔與其他破舊的圖畫書和一大堆垃圾，一起被扔進大袋子裡，帶往花園盡頭的雞舍後面。那是個點火焚燒東西的好地方，只是園丁太忙了，沒有時間馬上處理這些東西。他必須去挖馬鈴薯和摘豆子，不過他答應隔天一早會盡快把這些垃圾燒掉。

那天晚上，男孩睡在另一個房間，有隻新兔子陪伴他。那是隻很漂亮的兔子，全身的絨毛又白又長，有真正的玻璃眼珠。但是男孩不怎麼喜歡他，因為明天他就要去海邊，他滿腦子只想著這件美好的事。

就在男孩熟睡、夢見海邊的時候，小絨毛兔躺在一堆破舊的圖

畫書中，一起被放在雞舍後面的角落，他好孤單。袋口開著，他鑽來鑽去，把頭伸出袋口向外張望。他打了個寒顫，因為他一向都睡在溫暖又舒服的床上，加上他一身的天鵝絨毛已經被抱得又薄又破，沒有任何禦寒效果了。他看看四周，到處都是高高的覆盆子灌木，看起來就像熱帶叢林，在它們的樹蔭下，是他和男孩共度許多上午遊戲時光的地方。他想到陽光長時間照映花園的情景——那時候他們多麼快樂呀——心中不禁難過起來，他彷彿看見一切從眼前消失了，那些美好的時光；花床上的美麗小茅屋；安靜的傍晚躺在森林裡的蕨類上面，看著小螞蟻在他的腳掌間來回穿梭；還有他

第一次知道自己變成真的那天的美妙情景。他想起聰明又溫柔的真皮馬，想起他說的每句話。那些過去曾經被愛，並且因此失去美麗外貌而變成真實的東西，是不是都有這樣的下場？一顆淚珠，真正的淚珠，悄悄滑過他髒髒的絨毛鼻子，落到地上。

就在那時候，發生了一件奇妙的事。在淚水滴落的地方長出了一株花，充滿神祕色彩的花，和花園裡的花完全不一樣。它有鮮綠色的細長葉片，枝葉間開出了一朵像金杯的花，美得讓小絨毛兔忘了哭泣，只是呆呆看著它。花朵盛開了，裡面竟然出現一位仙子！

6

可_{ㄎㄜˇ}愛_{ㄞˋ}的_{ㄉㄜ˙}小_{ㄒㄧㄠˇ}仙_{ㄒㄧㄢ}子_{ㄗˇ}

她是全世界最可愛的小仙子，穿著珍珠和露珠裝飾的衣裳，頸子和頭髮上都圍著鮮花，她的臉更像一朵最美麗的花。她走向小絨毛兔，伸手扶起他，還在已經被他哭濕的絨毛鼻子上親了一下。

「小兔子，」她說。「你不知道我是誰嗎？」

絨毛兔仰起頭看著仙子，他彷彿見過這張臉，卻怎麼也想不起來在哪裡看過。「我就是育兒室的魔法仙子，」她說。「負責照顧那些孩子們深愛的玩具。當他們變得又舊又破，小孩再也不需要他們的時候，我就會來接他們，並且把他們變成真的。」

「難道我以前不是真的嗎？」小絨毛兔問。

「對男孩來說是真的，」仙子說，「因為他愛你。但是現在，你對每個人來說都會是真的了。」

說完，她便把小絨毛兔抱在懷裡，帶著他飛進森林。

月光把大地染得一片銀白，森林變得好美好美，蕨類的葉片也閃爍銀白色的光芒。一群野兔正在林間天鵝絨般的草地上和自己的影子跳舞，但是他們一見到仙子就紛紛停下來，站成圓圈注視著她。

「我為你們帶來一位新玩伴，」仙子說。「你們要好好待他，還要教他兔子王國需要知道的每件事，因為他要永遠和你們住

她又親親小兔子，把他放在草地上。

「快跑呀，小兔子，和他們一起玩吧！」她說。

小兔子只是靜靜坐著，動也不動一下。因為他看見那些野兔圍著他跳舞時，突然想起自己沒有後腿的事，他不想讓那些兔子看見自己的底部被縫成一整塊。但是，他不知道就在仙子最後一次親吻他的時候，也澈底改變了他。他害羞得不敢亂動，不知道坐了多久，小兔子突然覺得鼻子好癢好癢，他想都沒想就抬起後腿搔癢。然後，他發現自己真的有後腿了！他不再是又破又髒的絨毛

兔，他有棕色的毛，柔軟又閃亮，他的耳朵會自己抖動，鬍鬚長

得垂到草地。他輕輕跳了一下，然後興奮地用後腿在草地上蹦蹦跳

跳，像別的兔子一樣，一會兒跳向旁邊，一會兒繞圈圈。他實在太

高興了，等他停下來尋找仙子時，她已經不見了。

他終於變成真正的兔子，和其他的兔子住在一起。

秋天走了，冬天也跟著遠離，在陽光普照的溫暖春天，男孩

走進屋子後方的森林玩耍。他正玩得高興時，兩隻兔子鑽出那叢蕨

類，探出頭看著他。其中一隻全身棕色，可是另一隻身上的毛有

奇特的斑點，那些斑點好像很久很久以前就存在了，到現在依稀可

天鵝絨毛兔

見。還有他柔軟的小鼻子和那雙黑眼珠，看起來好熟悉，男孩在心中暗想：

「喔，他看起來好像我得猩紅熱時搞丟的那隻舊兔兔！」

然而，男孩永遠不會知道那正是自己的兔兔。他特別回到這裡，看看這個第一個使他成真的男孩。

我們每一個人其實也都是天鵝絨毛兔

◎恩佐

坦白說，我真的頗喜歡這篇故事。這讓我想起那些愛過我的人，還有自己那個曾經渴望被愛的脆弱靈魂。

剛收到文字稿的時候，看著標題「天鵝絨毛兔」，附帶上簡短的故事，我以為那是一本兒童讀物。

雖然我也期待能作兒童繪本，但考慮到手頭上大量的欠稿以

074

及目前的健康與心理狀態，創作一本負責任的兒童讀物，我的第一

個念頭是，目前似乎還不是時候。但基於職業道德，我想要拒絕也

得有個充分理由，至少得把文章看完，再告知編輯原因。於是我去

冰箱倒了一杯可樂，打算在氣泡揮發完之前，喝光它，並且看完所

有的篇章。只是當我開始進入天鵝絨毛兔的故事情節裡，那畫面就

像氣泡一樣漂浮上來，那不僅僅是職業上習慣性地畫面發想，而是

想起生命中每一個深刻卻又充滿模糊痕跡的溫暖時光。

我開始好奇故事的發展，可樂裡的氣泡繼續揮發，而我的腦

袋裡已經被一幅幅生動的畫面填滿，絨毛兔的故事相當簡潔卻又

不失豐富，他的每一個心境轉折，似乎都可以與真實世界相連結而

易於理解。我似乎頗能被說服在絨毛兔的故事裡，我喜歡他的結

局，老實說，它讓一部看似平凡的作品發亮了。

看完了稿子，我終於找到了理由，不過卻是接下這份工作的

理由。我暗自竊想，如果絨毛兔是虛構的，那我能做的，就是用畫

面讓他活出來。

某一種程度上，其實我們正扮演著小男孩。我自己有收集玩

具的嗜好，在沒有興趣的人眼裡，那不過只是一塊塑膠、鐵塊，但

是我卻愛不釋手。在我的心裡，它們絕不是一個冷冰冰毫無生命的

工廠製造品。但另一種程度上，我們每一個人其實也都是天鵝絨毛兔。我們的肉體，在經歷了愛與被愛之前，不也只是科學名詞上一堆原子分子的組合體，然而，因為情感的甜美與苦澀，我們獲得靈魂，最後取得生命的完整。

最後我還是想說，我喜歡作者用美好的情節來作為故事的結尾，她安慰了我因為分離而無法釋懷的傷悲。